PUFF...

Aussie Nibbles

Daryl's Dinner

Daryl, the baby magpie, has to
find his own food. But how,
when it's *so* easy to make
disgusting mistakes?

which Aussie Nibbles have you read?

 DARYL'S DINNER
Written and illustrated by
Catherine Jinks

 FOLLOW THAT LION!
Rosemary Hayes
Illustrated by Stephen Michael King

 SCRUFFY'S DAY OUT
Rachel Flynn
Illustrated by Jocelyn Bell

 CINDERFELLA
Dianne Bates
Illustrated by Peter Viska

 SNOWMAN MAGIC
Justin D'Ath
Illustrated by Emma Quay

 THE LITTLEST PIRATE
Sherryl Clark
Illustrated by Tom Jellett

Aussie Nibbles

Daryl's Dinner

Written and illustrated by
Catherine Jinks

Puffin Books

Puffin Books

Published by the Penguin Group
Penguin Books Australia Ltd
250 Camberwell Road
Camberwell, Victoria 3124, Australia
Penguin Books Ltd
80 Strand, London WC2R 0RL, England
Penguin Putnam Inc.
375 Hudson Street, New York, New York 10014, USA
Penguin Books Canada Limited
10 Alcorn Avenue, Toronto, Ontario, Canada, M4V 3B2
Penguin Books (N.Z.) Ltd
Cnr Rosedale and Airborne Roads, Albany, Auckland, New Zealand
Penguin Books (South Africa) (Pty) Ltd
24 Sturdee Avenue, Rosebank, Johannesburg 2196, South Africa
Penguin Books India (P) Ltd
11, Community Centre, Panchsheel Park, New Delhi 110 017, India

First published by Penguin Books Australia, 2002

3 5 7 9 10 8 6 4 2

Typeset in New Century School Book by Post Pre-press Group,
Brisbane, Queensland
Printed and bound in Australia by McPherson's Printing Group,
Maryborough, Victoria

Designed by Melissa Fraser, Penguin Design Studio
Series designed by Melissa Fraser
Series editor: Kay Ronai

National Library of Australia
Cataloguing-in-Publication data:
Jinks, Catherine, 1963– .
Daryl's dinner.
ISBN 0 14 131335 8.
1. Magpies – Juvenile fiction. I. Title. (Series: Aussie nibbles).
A823.3

www.puffin.com.au

To my mum, the birdwatcher

Chapter One

There were seven magpies.

Mum and Dad were big
and shiny, with black-and-
white feathers. Bob and Pip
were skinny and cross.

Lara, Kiki and Daryl
were the youngest. They

had lots of fluffy grey
feathers, and they were
always, *always* hungry.
'I'm hungry!' they would
scream. 'I'm *h-u-u-u-ngry!*'

They would flutter their wings, and open their big, pink mouths, and Mum and Dad would come running with food.

Mum would stuff a tasty caterpillar down Kiki's throat.

'Gulp!'

Dad would do the same for Lara.

'Gulp!'

Then Pip and Bob would flutter *their* wings. 'I'm hungry! I'm *hu-u-u-ungry*! I'm *HU-U-UNGRY*!' they would scream.

But Pip and Bob were
more than a year old. They
were too old to be fed. Their
mum and dad just ignored
them.

Pip and Bob had to find
their own food.

'You wait,' they told Lara
and Kiki and Daryl. 'Soon
Mum and Dad won't come
running when you call.

Soon, *you'll* have to run

after *them*.'

   And they were right,

because . . .

Chapter Two

. . . one day, the magpies
were wandering over a big
patch of grass, looking for
food. Lara was getting
hungry. She saw her
mother stop, and peck at
something.

So she began to scream.

'I'm hungry! I'm
hu-u-ungry!' she cried,
flapping her wings.

But her mother kept on
walking!

'Mu-um!' she screeched.

'M-u-um, I'm hungry!

I'm *hu-u-ungry!*'

Still her mother kept
walking.

'There. You see?' said Pip.

'I told you. Now *you'll* have to run after *them.*'

'And soon you'll have to find your own food,' Bob added in a grumpy voice.

'Find our own food?!'
shrieked Lara. 'But we
can't! We can't find our own
food!'

'You can if you're
starving,' Bob replied.

'But I *am* starving! I'm starving *now*!' said Lara, and scurried after her mum and dad, fluttering her wings madly. 'Mu-um! *Mu-u-um*!

You have to feed me! I'm starving! *MU-U-UM*!'

'Just wait,' said her mother.

'But Mu-u-um –'

'Just *wait!*'

Now Kiki started
screaming too. They both
danced about, screaming
and fluttering their wings.

Daryl didn't join them. He stood for a while, watching. He thought, I wonder how you find your own food?

Then he strolled away into some bushes . . .

Chapter Three

... where lots and lots of things were scattered over the ground.

They all looked delicious.

'Yum,' said Daryl, and picked something up in his beak.

It was brown and red and
black and grey.

He tried to swallow it,
but . . .

'OW!'

It bit his tongue!

'*Ow*! Ow-ow-ow-ow!' he cried. '*Yeo-o-o-w*!' He ran out of the bushes.

'What is it?' asked Pip.

'What happened?' asked Bob.

'It hurts! It hurts!' yelped
Daryl. 'It bit me!'

Bob and Pip looked down
at what Daryl had dropped.
Then they laughed.

'It didn't bite you, it burnt you!' said Pip. 'That's a cigarette butt!'

'You silly bird,' said Bob. 'You can't eat cigarette butts.'

They walked off, still
laughing, as they searched
the ground for their dinner.
Daryl followed them. His
tongue was cooling down
and he was getting hungry.

'Go away,' Bob told him.
'We're busy. We're looking
for worms, and we don't
want you around.'

'Why not?' asked Daryl.

'Because you're too

young, and you're too
stupid,' Bob replied. 'Only
stupid birds eat cigarette
butts.' He snapped at Daryl
with his long, sharp beak.
'Go away!'

So Daryl went. He headed
for a shady, wet spot under
some trees. Pecking and
poking, he started to look
for worms. And . . .

Chapter Four

. . . he found one!

It was long and slimy.

It was hiding in the dirt.

It wriggled when he picked

it up.

'Gulp!' He swallowed it.

But then something

strange happened.

He couldn't open his beak.
It felt sticky. It was stuck.
He rubbed it on the ground.
He scraped it on a tree.

He shook it until it
clattered. Little balls of
slime began to fly around.

'M-m-mm!' he wailed.
'Dd-d-d!'

He ran over to where his

parents stood. They were

flicking through a pile of

dead leaves. Kiki and Lara

were with them.

'M-m-m! D-d-d-d!' cried

Daryl.

'Oh, Daryl,' Mum groaned.
'Did you eat a slug?'

'A thlug?' said Daryl
thickly. He couldn't talk
properly because of the
slime on his tongue.

'You shouldn't eat slugs,
you silly bird,' said Dad.
'You'll get slimed.'

'Ha-ha! Ha-ha! Daryl ate
a slu-ug!' cried Kiki.

'Go and scrape it off on

the grass,' said Mum. 'Go
on. And stop being so silly.
I'll feed you, Daryl. You just
have to wait your turn.'

But I'm *not* being silly,

Daryl thought, as he wiped
his beak on the wet grass.
I just want to find my own
food.

Looking over at Kiki and
Lara, who were screaming
and flapping again, he
knew that he would soon

get very, very hungry if he
didn't find something to
eat. So . . .

Chapter Five

. . . he decided to search the

driveway.

It was flat and white,

and covered with cracks.

Daryl began to follow one

of the bigger cracks. Surely

he would find something . . .

Then he stopped. He
could see food. It was fat.
It was brown. It looked like
the sausage that his mum
and dad had found beside
a rubbish bin one day.

A sausage! Another
sausage!

'Yippee!' Daryl cried.
He picked up a chunk of
sausage, and swallowed it.
It tasted a bit funny.

It didn't taste like the other
sausage.

But that didn't bother
him much. He was too
proud of having found

a real sausage to worry
about what it tasted like.

'Mum! Dad!' he shouted.
'Come quickly! I've found
a sausage!'

The other birds came
running. They all loved
sausage.

'Where? Where?' said Pip.

'Show me!' said Mum.

'I want some!' said Kiki.

'Now stand back,
children,' Dad ordered.
'Daryl, where's the
sausage?'

Daryl showed him. Dad gasped.

'Daryl,' he said, 'did you *eat* any of that?'

'Yes,' Daryl replied. 'But just a bit.'

'Oh, Daryl,' said Dad. 'That's not a sausage. That's *dog-poo*!'

Chapter Six

Pip and Bob fell about
laughing. Kiki and Lara
shrieked.

'Daryl ate dog-poo! Daryl
ate dog-poo!' they cackled.

'Now, children, stop it,'
said Mum.

'Daryl ate dog-poo!'

'That's enough,' said Dad.
'Daryl, wash your mouth
out. And *don't* eat dog-poo
ever again.'

Sadly, Daryl slouched off
to find some water. He felt
very, very stupid. He also
felt a bit sick.

There was water in a big

flowerpot near the compost
bin. He jumped up onto
the rim of the flowerpot,
swished his beak through
the water, and gargled.

Then he saw something.
It was lying on the
ground near the compost
bin. It was white. It was big.
Daryl went to investigate.

'That looks like bread,'
he thought. He sniffed at it.
He poked at it. He peered
at it.

Then he picked it up,
carefully, and dragged it

over to his mum and dad.

'Why, Daryl!' said Mum,
staring in amazement. 'Is
that bread you've got?'

'Daryl!' Dad exclaimed.
'You clever, clever bird!'
They looked at each
other. They looked at Daryl.

Kiki began to flap her
wings.

'I want some! I wa-a-ant
some!' she cried.

'I want some too!'

screamed Lara.

'No,' said Mum firmly.

'That bread is Daryl's.

He found it, so he can eat it.

That's what happens when

you find your own food.'

'But, Mum, I'm hungry!'
Kiki whined.

'So am I!' said Lara.

'I'm hungry! I'm hungry!

I'm hungry!' Bob and Pip
and Lara and Kiki all
wailed.

Daryl stepped forward.

'It's all right,' he told them.

'It's a big piece of bread. There's enough for everyone.'

And there was. And everyone had a bite. But Daryl should have eaten it all, because . . .

. . . Lara and Kiki and Pip and Bob are always chasing after *him* now!

From Catherine Jinks

I've always liked magpies. They have such character – especially baby ones. I love the way they mooch around, and whinge, and play with each other. I've even seen baby magpies wrestling.

But I've never really seen one try to eat dog-poo. They're quite clever birds. I don't think even a *baby* magpie would be *that* stupid.

Want another nibble?

Aussie Nibbles

The Littlest Pirate

Sherryl Clark
Illustrated by Tom Jellett

Nicholas Nosh is the littlest pirate in the
world. His family won't let him go to sea
and he's bored. 'I'll show them,' he says.

Follow That Lion!

Rosemary Hayes
Illustrated by Stephen Michael King

Hector's mum has found an
unusual pet. She says it is gentle.
Hector knows better . . .

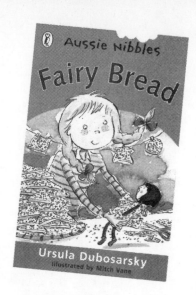

Fairy Bread

Ursula Dubosarsky
Illustrated by Mitch Vane

Becky only wants fairy bread at
her party. But there's so much left
over, and she won't throw it out.

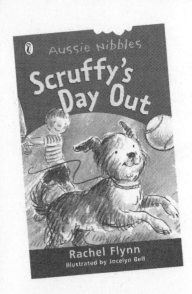

Scruffy's Day Out

Rachel Flynn
Illustrated by Jocelyn Bell

Dad saves a scruffy little
dog from being run over.
But whose dog is it?

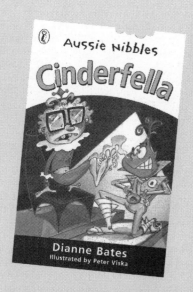

Cinderfella

Dianne Bates
Illustrated by Peter Viska

What happens when Cinderfella,
of the Planet Jetsonia, meets Princess
Esmerelda of the Planet Earth?

It is Kerry's first day
at her new school.
Will she find a friend?

Crystal longs to be a
mermaid. So her mother
makes her a special tail.

Anna had never slept over at a
friend's house. Until now . . .
Was she brave enough?

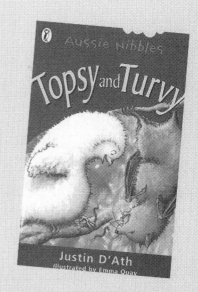

Why are Topsy and Turvy
so different?
One day they learn why.

It's Saturday morning. Auskick is about to start. But Brendan thinks his pet fish is sick.

Their grandmother loved blue. She also hated her grey hair. Sonya and Margo knew what to do

Benny loves the dog that lives nearby. But why is it so sad?

Becky's two gorillas were very scary. Until they had their first bath.